Put Beginning Readers on the Right Track with
ALL ABOARD READING™

The All Aboard Reading series is especially designed for beginning readers. Written by noted authors and illustrated in full color, these are books that children really want to read—books to excite their imagination, expand their interests, make them laugh, and support their feelings. With fiction and nonfiction stories that are high interest and curriculum-related, All Aboard Reading books offer something for every young reader. And with four different reading levels, the All Aboard Reading series lets you choose which books are most appropriate for your children and their growing abilities.

Picture Readers

Picture Readers have super-simple texts, with many nouns appearing as rebus pictures. At the end of each book are 24 flash cards—on one side is a rebus picture; on the other side is the written-out word.

Station Stop 1

Station Stop 1 books are best for children who have just begun to read. Simple words and big type make these early reading experiences more comfortable. Picture clues help children to figure out the words on the page. Lots of repetition throughout the text helps children to predict the next word or phrase—an essential step in developing word recognition.

Station Stop 2

Station Stop 2 books are written specifically for children who are reading with help. Short sentences make it easier for early readers to understand what they are reading. Simple plots and simple dialogue help children with reading comprehension.

Station Stop 3

Station Stop 3 books are perfect for children who are reading alone. With longer text and harder words, these books appeal to children who have mastered basic reading skills. More complex stories captivate children who are ready for more challenging books.

In addition to All Aboard Reading books, look for All Aboard Math Readers™ (fiction stories that teach math concepts children are learning in school); All Aboard Science Readers™ (nonfiction books that explore the most fascinating science topics in age-appropriate language); and All Aboard Poetry Readers™ (funny, rhyming poems for readers of all levels).

All Aboard for happy reading!

To Tom and Kathy Brennan's sweet bunch—
Matthew, Mark, and Kaitlin
—P.D.

To my nieces and nephews—J.D.

Special thanks to Paul L. Sieswerda, Curator, Aquarium for Wildlife
Conservation, New York.

Text copyright © 1995 by Patricia Demuth. Illustrations copyright © 1995 by Jim Deal. All
rights reserved. Published by Grosset & Dunlap, a division of Penguin Young Readers Group,
345 Hudson Street, New York, NY 10014. GROSSET & DUNLAP and ALL ABOARD
SCIENCE READER are trademarks of Penguin Group (USA) Inc. Published simultaneously
in Canada. Printed in the U.S.A.

Library of Congress Cataloging-in-Publication Data

Demuth, Patricia.
     Way down deep / by Patricia Demuth ; illustrated by Jim Deal.
          p.   cm. — (All aboard reading)
     "Level 2, grades 1-3."
     1. Oceanography—Juvenile literature.   [1. Oceanography.]   I. Deal, Jim, 1956-   ill.
II. Title. III. Series.
     GC21.5.D46   1995
     551.46—dc20   94-39040
                                                                                  CIP
                                                                                   AC

ISBN 0-448-40851-1   L M N O P Q R S T

Way Down Deep

Strange Ocean Creatures

By Patricia Demuth
Illustrated by Jim Deal

Grosset & Dunlap • New York

Long, long ago,
explorers first sailed
across the Atlantic Ocean.

5

The trip was scary.

There were tales

of strange monsters—

mermaids, serpents,
and sea dragons that could
snap a ship in two.

Of course, there were no monsters.

But the ocean <u>is</u> full of strange creatures.

Today explorers go down,

down,

down,

into the deepest parts of the sea.

What they find is more amazing

than any of the old tales.

The ocean bottom is like another world.

In some places it is flat for miles.

In other places there are steep mountains.

Sometimes the mountaintops
rise out of the water.
These are islands.

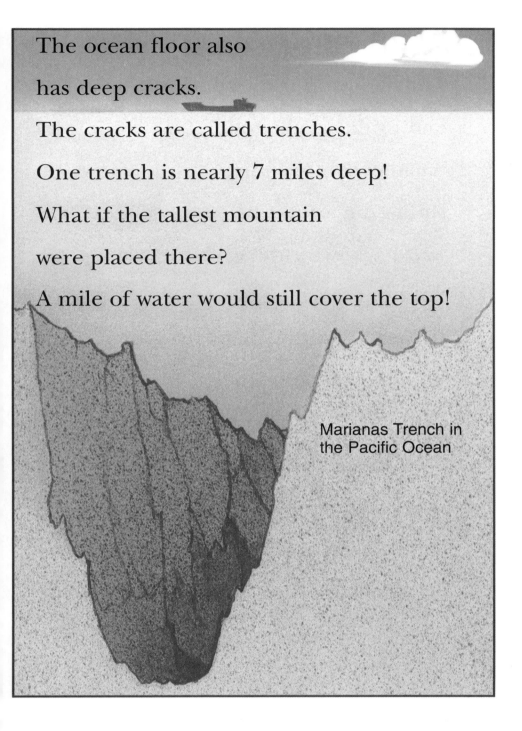

The ocean floor also

has deep cracks.

The cracks are called trenches.

One trench is nearly 7 miles deep!

What if the tallest mountain

were placed there?

A mile of water would still cover the top!

Marianas Trench in
the Pacific Ocean

We think of the ocean as blue.

But the water is only blue

and bright at the top.

That's because sunlight

shines down into it.

Farther down, the water gets darker.

Sunlight fades away.

It is too dark for plants to grow.

Finally, way down deep,

there is no light at all.

The ocean is black there.

It is cold, too—icy cold.

That's because the deep, deep waters

get almost no heat from the sun.

How do we know what it is like

in the deep ocean?

Even in special suits,

divers can't go down very far.

So scientists must find other ways.

They use little underwater boats.

They are called <u>submersibles</u>.

(You say it like this: sub-MER-si-bulls.)

Ships carry submersibles out to sea.

Then they are put overboard.

This is a famous submersible
named Alvin.

Alvin can carry three people.

It has lots of tools to do many jobs.

A floodlight lights up the dark sea.

Cameras take pictures.

A steel claw picks up things
from the ocean floor.

A probe takes the temperature
of the water.

A "vacuum cleaner" collects
sea creatures.

Alvin can dive down 14,000 feet.
Scientists use robots
to explore deeper water.

Robots can go where people cannot.

They can even go into

the deepest trenches.

The pictures they take show

what these places are like.

All these creatures live

in the deep sea.

You can see that many have

huge mouths and sharp teeth.

Food is hard to find in the dark.

When a meal passes by,

the fish are ready to grab it.

20

Many deepwater fish have lights
on their bodies.
Lights help fish find their mates
in the dark.
They also help fish to get food.

This is a deep-sea angler.

A light dangles from the top

of its head.

It looks like bait at the end

of a fishing rod.

A fish swims by.

It thinks the light is a bit of food.

GULP! The angler has dinner.

The gulper eel has a red light
at the end of its tail.

The viperfish has lights
right inside its mouth.

25

Many squid live in the deep sea.

Some squid give off light, too.

This is a jeweled squid.

It has twenty-two lights

that sparkle like jewels.

The vampire squid looks like
it wears a black cape.
Its red eyes glow in the dark.

The biggest deep-sea animal of all
is the giant squid.
It can grow more than 60 feet long!
Its huge green eyes are bigger
than a man's fist.

30

Sperm whales don't live in the deep sea.

But they are deep divers.

They come down to hunt

the giant squid.

A battle breaks out.
The giant squid wraps
its long arms and tentacles
around the sperm whale.

Its suckers cut into the whale.

Then the squid gets away.

Many animals make their home
right on the ocean floor.
Sea slugs creep about
on one small foot.

Tripod fish walk along the bottom.

They look like they have three legs.

But really the legs are fins.

These animals leave tracks

on the ocean floor-

just like animals do on land.

The sea cucumber sucks up mud
like a vacuum cleaner sucks up dirt.
There is a lot of good food in the mud.

Sometimes currents
stir up the mud.
Then there's a mud storm!
Bits of food fly everywhere.
The animals have a feast!

37

Other deep-sea animals wait for food

to fall down from above.

A rain of food is always falling

in the sea.

It comes from dead animals.

The food sinks down, down, down

to the icy-cold bottom.

Dark and cold—

that's what most

of the ocean bottom is like.

But there are hot spots, too.

Here the water is boiling hot.

How can that be?

At some places,

the ocean bottom is heated

by hot melted rocks called lava.

Lava comes from deep inside the earth.

It pushes through cracks

in the ocean bottom.

The lava heats the seawater,

just like a stove burner heats

water in a teapot.

The water can heat up to 700 degrees!

Sometimes minerals in the hot water
form large chimneys.
These chimneys can be as high as
a two-story house!

The water gushing out of the chimneys

is as black as smoke.

It is a strange sight to see

a row of smoking chimneys

on the ocean floor!

A zoo of odd creatures live here.

Giant worms cling to the chimneys.

Some have bright-red tips that reach

out from white cases.

On the rocks near the chimneys

are spider crabs.

They are as big as dinner plates.

Huge clams also settle near

the super-hot water.

Rich metals can be found here, too—
gold, silver, and copper.
Right now it is too hard
to dig them out.
But maybe one day we will
mine the ocean bottom.

Exploring the deep sea is like
a big treasure hunt.
Scientists discover new things every day
about the huge, watery world
way down deep!